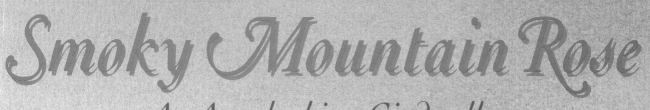

Smoky Mountain Rose
An Appalachian Cinderella

by
ALAN SCHROEDER

pictures by
BRAD SNEED

Dial Books for Young Readers / New York

For Bob San Souci, a terrific storyteller and a good friend
—A.S.

For Emily
—B.S.

Published by Dial Books for Young Readers
A Division of Penguin Books USA Inc.
375 Hudson Street
New York, New York 10014

Text copyright © 1997 by Alan Schroeder
Pictures copyright © 1997 by Bradley D. Sneed
All rights reserved
Designed by Nancy R. Leo
Printed in Hong Kong
First Edition
1 3 5 7 9 10 8 6 4 2

Library of Congress Cataloging in Publication Data
Schroeder, Alan.
Smoky Mountain Rose : an Appalachian Cinderella /
by Alan Schroeder ; pictures by Brad Sneed.
p.   cm.
Based on Charles Perrault's Cendrillon.
Summary: In this variation on the Cinderella story, based on the Charles Perrault
version but set in the Smoky Mountains, Rose loses her glass slipper at
a party given by the rich feller on the other side of the creek.
ISBN 0-8037-1733-4.—ISBN 0-8037-1734-2 (lib. bdg.)
[1. Fairy tales. 2. Folklore—France.] I. Sneed, Brad, ill.
II. Perrault, Charles, 1628–1703. Cendrillon. III. Cinderella. English. IV. Title.
PZ8.S3125Sm 1997   398.21'09768'89—dc20   [E]   92-1250   CIP   AC

The artwork was prepared with watercolor.

ᘛᘚ Author's Note ᘛᘚ

The story of *Cinderella* is one of the most popular and well-known of all fairy tales. It is also one of the oldest: Its roots can be traced back to China, circa 850 A.D. For Western readers, the most familiar retelling of *Cinderella* is Charles Perrault's "Cendrillon," which was published in Paris in 1697. It is upon this version that I have based my own story, *Smoky Mountain Rose*.

American versions of the tale abound. "Catskins," "Ashpet," and "Rush Cape" (or "Cap o' Rushes") are all dialect retellings (the latter mingles the stories of *Cinderella* and *King Lear*). In "Ashpet," the heroine is not part of the family, but a "hired girl," and her great dream is to go to the church meeting, not the palace ball. The fairy godmother is a peculiar old witch-woman, and near the end of the story the wicked sisters take Ashpet to "the swimmin' place," where she is caught by the "Old Hairy Man" who inhabits the lake.

"Catskins" is unique, not for its use of dialect, but for its unsympathetic heroine. At no point does Catskins seem to be a victim; she comes across as self-centered, untrustworthy, and materialistic. The stepsister, on the other hand, is presented as kindly and generous, even lending Catskins a dress for the "big dance at the King's house."

"Ashpet" and "Catskins" can be found in Richard Chase's delightful *Grandfather Tales* (Houghton Mifflin, 1948). "Rush Cape" appears in Chase's *American Folk Tales and Songs* (New American Library of World Literature, 1956). Finally, an interesting overview of *Cinderella* can be found in *The Classic Fairy Tales* by Iona and Peter Opie (Oxford University Press, 1974).

Now lis'en.

Smack in the heart o' the Smoky Mountains, there was this old trapper livin' in a log cabin with his daughter. One night, while Rose was fryin' a mess o' fish, the trapper, he starts lookin' dejected-like.

"I reckon it's hard on ye, not havin' a ma," he said. "Tell me, Rose, would ye lak me to git hitched again? There's a widow woman with two daughters down the road a piece. Way I see it, we'd all fit together neater'n a jigsaw."

"I don't mind," said Rose, settin' a plate o' corn bread on the table. "You go a-courtin', Pa, if you think it's best."

So before the huckleberries was fit for pickin', the trapper got himself hitched for the second time. That's when the trouble started a-brewin'.

Ye see, Gertie, the new wife, she was just about the crossest, fearsomest woman that side o' Tarbelly Creek. And her two daughters—why, they were so mean they'd steal flies from a blind spider. And vain? Them girls could waste a whole day admirin' themselves in the mirror.

"Ain't I purty?" Annie would say, peering into the glass.

"Not as purty as me!" Liza Jane would retort. "Y'all watch, someday I'm gonna marry me a fine gentleman—go to Memphis and live lak a lady!"

Rose, on the other hand, was a sweet li'l thing, always lookin' out for others and takin' care of sick critters, and the like. Annie and Liza Jane couldn't stand the sight of her. To be orn'ry, they dressed her in the sorriest-lookin' rags and made her do plumb near every chore.

Well, it just about broke the trapper's heart to see his daughter out milkin' the cow and collectin' the firewood and churnin' the butter. He woulda talked to Gertie 'bout it, but talkin' to her was like kickin' an agitated rattler. The trapper figgered it was best to say nothin' at all.

This went on for a long time. Then one day the trapper up and died. Rose had loved her pa somethin' fierce, and for days on end she couldn't stop a-weepin'.

Finally Gertie lit into her, mean as a hornet. "Shet up that cryin'," she screeched, "or I'm gonna feed ye t' the dogs, ye hear?"

From then on, Rose's life was just about as hard as it could be. Chores from sunup t' sundown. Course, she thought of runnin' away, but she didn't have anywhere to go. She figgered she just had to set it out and wait for a better day to come 'long.

Now it so happens that on the other side o' the creek, there was this real rich feller—made his fortune in sowbellies and grits. Well, this feller wasn't hitched yet, so one day he gets the bright idea to invite all the neighbor-people to a fancy ol' party, thinkin' he might find himself a wife. When Annie and Liza Jane got their invitation, they plumb near went crazy with excitement.

"I'm gonna order me a brand-new dress out of that there catalog!" Annie declared.

"No, you ain't!" cried Liza Jane. "That cat'log is mine, you skunk! Take your hands off it!"

Now Rose, she sorta figgered she was invited too. When Annie and Liza Jane heard that, they started a-howlin': "Lawd-a-marcy! Who'd want to dance with a dirt clod lak you?"

For the next few days they worked Rose like they was fixin' to kill her. A full hour before the sun was up, she'd be ironin' their dresses and polishin' their shoes and every other durn fool thing. Now Rose, she wanted to go to the party somethin' awful, but she held her tongue for fear of bein' laughed at again.

The actual night of the shindig the two sisters were downright hateful.

"Hand me that comb, stupid!"

"Tie up my hair ribbon!"

"Whar's my corset?"

Rose ran left and right, tryin' to keep up with their demands. Finally, toward seven o'clock, Gertie and her daughters piled into the tater wagon. Whippin' the mule, they went a-rumblin' down the dirt road, chortlin' out "Skip t' M' Lou" at the top of their lungs.

Rose, meanwhile, sat next to the pigsty and cried. Far off 'cross the creek she could hear the sound of fiddle music. That made her cry even harder.

Just then one of the hogs comes moseyin' up to the fence and starts talkin' to her.

"Ye shore look mis'rable, honey. But don't ye fret none. I know magic and I kin help."

Rose, she just stared, figgerin' she'd done lost her wits. But the hog kept right on talkin'.

"First of all, we gotta get ye out o' them rags. Now stand up and turn around real fast, like ye got a whompus cat bitin' at yer britches."

Rose did just what the hog told her. When she looked down, she was wearin' the purtiest party dress she ever laid eyes on.

"I must be dreamin'," she said to herself.

The hog studied her real careful-like. "Lookin' good, sister—but time's a-wastin'. We gotta get ye over to that shindig. Go fetch me a mushmelon and two field mice."

Again, Rose did just what she was told.

"Now watch," said the hog, and directly the mushmelon was turned into a big ol' wagon. And the mice? Two strong horses, with silky manes and shiny teeth—real show critters.

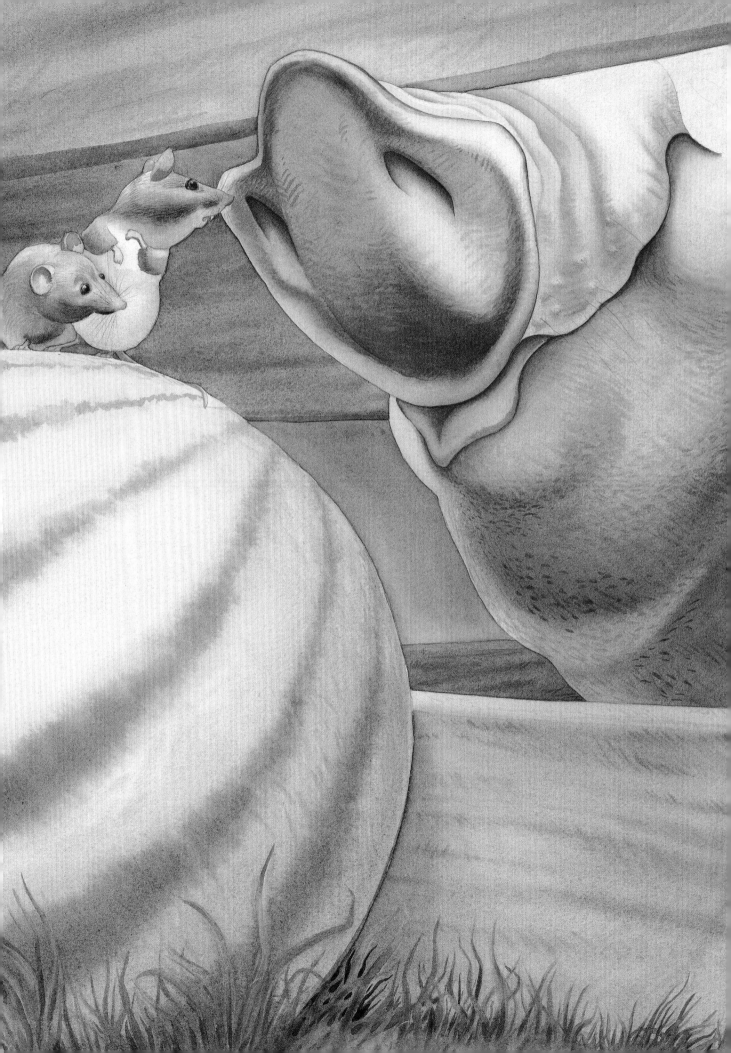

Rose was thrilled t' pieces. She was all set to hop up on the wagon, when the hog let out a big snort. "Why, look at them filthy bare feet! That won't do t'all. Close your eyes. . . . Now open 'em."

Rose looked down. On each foot, she was wearin' a sparklin' glass slipper.

"Ye like 'em?" asked the hog.

"Well," said Rose, tryin' to be polite, "they're not too pract'cal for square dancin', but they sure are purty."

The hog watched as Rose climbed up into the wagon.

"Now don't forget: The spell's only good till midnight, so ye gotta be home by then."

"I'll remember," said Rose, and off she went, a-rumblin' down the dirt road, just as happy as can be.

The shindig was even fancier than she'd reckoned. There were two
fiddlers, a harmonica man, even a square-dance caller come all the
way from Nashville. Everyone was dancin' and laughin' and drinkin'
cup after cup o' sarsaparilla.

Now the rich feller, he wasn't havin' such a good time. No one had
caught his fancy, see — and then, all of a sudden Rose came in through

the big barn door. She looked so purty that everyone stopped dead in their tracks. The two stepsisters, they pract'cally choked on their cider. "Well, shet my mouth!" one of 'em whispered. "How'd *she* get in here, and whar'd she git all them clothes?"

"I oughta wring her neck!" snapped the other. "She's been goin' through my bood-whar!"

They watched, jaws a-droppin', as the rich feller went hurryin' up to Rose, thrustin' out his hand. "Pleased to meet ye, missy," he said, real friendly. "My name's Seb. How 'bout takin' a turn round the dance floor?"

"My pleasure," said Rose, and off they went, arm in arm.

Neighbors cleared a space and watched as the two lovebirds started promenadin' to the tune o' "Baldy Holler."

> *"Eight hands up and go to the left,*
> *Backwards now, and home ye go!"*

All evenin' long, Rose and Seb kicked up their heels, havin' a high ol' time. Gertie and her two daughters stood off to the side, madder'n blazes. "Look at her," sneered Gertie, "sashayin' round lak she's the belly o' the ball. I'll fix her when she gits home—give her a list o' chores she won't never finish."

Just then Rose happened to glance at the big granddaddy clock in the corner.

"Tarnation!" she cried. "It's midnight!"

Without another word, she went dashin' out the barn door. Poor thing was runnin' so fast, one of her glass slippers went flyin' off into the dirt. She'd a-fetched it, but there warn't time.

"Come back!" cried Seb, chasin' after her. But Rose's wagon was already rattlin' down the road just as fast as it could go.

No sooner was she out o' sight than everythin' turned back the way it used t' be. The wagon was a mushmelon again, and Rose had to walk home dressed in rags. Only thing that hadn't changed was the remainin' glass slipper, which she tucked in her pocket for safe-keepin'.

Before goin' indoors, Rose stopped at the sty to say thank you.

"Anytime, sugar," said the hog.

Now Gertie and her daughters, they came tearin' home 'bout ten minutes later. Rose was already asleep by the fire.

"Ain't ye gonna whip her now, Ma?" said Liza Jane.

"My whippin' arm's tired. I'll do it tomorrow," said Gertie. "You gals git to bed now and git yer beauty sleep. Don't you worry—there'll be fireworks in the mornin'."

Sure enough, the next day Gertie lit into Rose somethin' awful. "Showin' up at that party, makin' my girls look lak fools!" she screeched. "I'll larn ye!" Grabbin' the switch, she was all set to whip Rose, when her two daughters came flyin' up the hill.

"Listen, Ma!" cried Annie. "That rich feller, he found Rose's shoe in the dirt, and now he's goin' round t' every house to find the owner!"

"And that ain't all!" said Liza Jane. "That feller, Ma, he's plumb crazy—says he's gettin' hitched with the first person it fits on, and I reckon it's gonna be me!"

"Well, then, harry up and git ready," said Gertie. "And listen, y'all, whichever of you gets the weddin' ring and moves to Memphis, I'm comin' along—ye ain't leavin' me behind!" Then, turnin' to Rose, Gertie warned: "You stay outta sight, or I'll blister yer rump somethin' fierce."

Half an hour later Seb came rattlin' up the road in his wagon. Gertie was there a-waitin' on the porch, shuckin' peas.

"Why, it's the sowbelly and grits feller," she said, actin' real surprised. "Come on in and set a spell. Understand ye found my daughter's shoe."

Before Seb had even said "Howdy-do," Annie came flyin' out on the porch, stickin' out her foot. "Me first!" she yelled, settin' herself down on a big milk bucket. Now Seb, he commences to tuggin' and pullin', but gettin' the slipper onto her big foot was like tryin' to stretch a li'l bitty sausage skin over a side o' beef.

"Git out o' my way," said Liza Jane, pushin' her sister aside. And right away she starts a-battin' her eyes at Seb. "I wanna thank ye for returnin' my shoe," she said. "I 'bout fell into a fidget o' fear when I saw it was gone." But Seb could tell she was just sweet-talkin'. The minute the tuggin' started, Liza Jane purt-near went blue in the face. "Lemme git the axe," she said, a-gaspin'. "I'll get that shoe on if it kills me!"

Just then Seb spotted Rose standin' off near the pigsty. "Warn't you at the shindig last night?" he called out.

Rose went on feedin' the hogs lak she didn't hear him.

"Come over here, and stick out yer foot," Seb told her. He watched as Rose came a-walkin' toward him. "You look mighty familiar, missy. Come on now, just set yerself down on this here bucket and stick out yer tootsie."

Annie and Liza Jane held their breath as Rose stretched out her pretty li'l foot. "Now hold still," Seb told her, and wouldn't ye know it, the slipper went glidin' right on, just as smooth as butter!

When Gertie saw that, she started a-screechin': "That weasel, she's a-trickin' ye! Why, my daughters are a heap purtier'n her!"

But Seb, he didn't pay her no mind—happy as a pig in a peanut patch, he took up Rose's hand and held it tight.

"I knew I'd find ye!" he whispered, and Rose nodded, all teary-eyed. Then, rememberin' the other slipper, she took it out of her pocket and put it on. Very same moment, the hog started snortin' and kickin' up a fuss, and when Rose looked down again, she was wearin' the exact same dress she had on at the shindig—lookin' just as purty as bluebonnets in spring.

'Pon seein' that, the two stepsisters, they done burst into tears. "Our precious li'l sister gonna be marryin' into money!" And they set to fussin' over her lak they jest loved her to pieces. Now Rose, she could have turned her back on 'em, but she didn't. Sweet thing, she figgered it was best t' fergive and forget.

"I love ye like soup loves salt," she told 'em, and from then on Annie and Liza Jane never gave 'er a moment o' grief or heartache.

And the weddin' that followed? Well, it was jest 'bout the biggest shindig ever seen in the Smoky Mountains. To this day, Rose and Seb are still livin' there, and folks reckon they're 'bout the happiest twosome in all o' Tarbelly Creek.